SKELETON IN THE CLOSET

AND OTHER SCARY STORIES

WRITTEN BY RUSSELL J. DORN

ILLUSTRATED BY DAVID VINCENT DORN

ISBN: ISBN - 9781976964930

Second Edition Print, January 2018. Black and white.

11 10 9 8 7 6 5 4 3 2

FOR THOSE WITH SKELETONS IN THEIR CLOSETS.

TABLE OF CONTENTS

SKELETON IN THE CLOSET

It started when Felipe got an F on his report card. Rather than bring the card to his parents, he buried it under a pile of several coats in his closet. He hoped they'd never find it. This might have been the end of it, if he hadn't come home to his father cleaning the following day.

"Thought I'd help you clean your closet next, Sport," his father said from behind the vacuum.

"That's all right, dad," Felipe said in an attempt to keep his father out of his closet. It would be nice to have help cleaning, but he had a secret to keep. "I can do it myself."

"Nonsense!" his father said. "I'm in a cleaning mood and many hands make light work. I'll be there in a minute."

After putting down his backpack, Felipe raced to his closet. Opening it, he jumped back, surprised. It might have been mistaken for a trick of the light or a Halloween decoration, but it wasn't. It was a real skeleton. The skeleton sat atop the pile of coats. In its bony hand was Felipe's report card.

"Tsk! Tsk!" the skeleton tapped the report card with the small bone of its index finger as it spoke. Even without lungs or a throat the skeleton had a heavy, breathy voice. The skeleton's speech was as broken as its bony body. It paused where it shouldn't have and broke the words up like the joints of its own frame—femur to tibia, mandible to cranium, 'skeleton' to 'ske'le'ton.' It was a little difficult to understand it at first. "An F in math'ma'tics? What a s'hame. Your fat'her will be an'gry."

Felipe felt a great fear of the talking skeleton, but strangely he felt more fear of his parents knowing his grades, as well as knowing he had hidden them.

"Don't wo'rry," the skeleton said. "I'll keep your se'cret for 'a s'in."

"My secret for a sin?"

"Yes, but you must ag'ree first."

"All right," Felipe said. "I agree."

Though the skeleton had no fleshy cheeks with which to do so, it seemed to smile. It said, "Knock that vase ov'er there to the fl'oor."

Felipe looked where the skeleton pointed. The vase was his mother's favorite. It stood atop a narrow table in the hall so that she could see it every day. It would not go unmissed.

"You'd bet'ter hu'rry," the skeleton said as Felipe shut the closet door on him.

The skeleton was right—Felipe didn't have much time. Just as he was darting out of his room, his father came down the hall. "Careful now, Felipe. No running," his father said and Felipe stopped running until his father rounded the corner; then he ran the rest of the way to the vase. Standing in front of the glass container, he wrestled with his new choice: break a vase and keep his secret, or save his mother the heartache of losing an heirloom and take his punishment for his bad grade.

His father entered Felipe's room.

He moved to the closet door.

He raised his hand to the closet handle—Felipe could hear its familiar rattle. Slowly, his father turned the handle.

CRASH!

The heirloom vase fell to the floor with a great shattering sound. Felipe's father came at once to see the damage. His face went white. The vase was in several dozen pieces.

"Sorry! I was running," Felipe lied, "and it fell over. I couldn't catch it."

His father sighed and took his own head into his hands. It seemed as if he was trying to keep his anger from escaping out of his ears. After a moment, he said, "Accidents happen. I'll clean this up. You get to work on your closet. A fully cleaned house might help your mother be less upset when she finds out."

Felipe did as he was told. It took him quite a while to get all of the coats and socks put away. The skeleton stood in the corner of the closet the entire time, watching. It still held the report card. As Felipe was finishing up vacuuming the closet, he heard his mother come in the front door. He could hear her -weep a little after speaking to his father. It was clear she'd been told about the vase. Then Felipe heard his mother walking towards his room. His heartbeat quickened.

With the closet clean, there was nowhere left to hide the report card, not to mention a full-sized skeleton! Besides, the skeleton still held the report card in its bony hands and didn't seem likely to give it up. The report card held power over Felipe, after all.

His mother's footsteps resounded from the hall.

"I'll keep your se'cret for 'a s'in," the skeleton said.

"All right!" Felipe said, urgently. "What is it? What would you have me do?"

"S'moke this cig'a'rette." The skeleton held out a lit cigarette. The smell of it infiltrated the closet in an instant. There would be no hiding it like he might be able to hide the F on his report card. Reluctantly, Felipe took the cigarette in his mouth. As he did, the Skeleton withdrew into the dark corner of the closet. The door opened and Felipe looked at his mother. Her mouth was wide open. Angrily, she snatched the cigarette and threw it in the nearby sink.

"What has gotten into you?" she said and set about digging through the dresser drawers looking for more cigarettes. "Where did you get that cigarette?"

Felipe had to think fast or she'd discover the skeleton in the closet—and his report card! "From Thomas next door! It was only the one."

She stopped digging through his sock drawer.

"We'll just see what he has to say about that," his mother said and walked away. She shouted from down the hall, "You're grounded!" A few minutes later she returned with Thomas. Thomas refused to admit he'd given Felipe the cigarette. He hadn't, after all, but Felipe had to get him to take the blame. Since their stories didn't line up, Felipe's mother told them to take a minute to talk it over and come to the truth. She left and Felipe brought Thomas into the closet to muffle their voices in case his mother was listening.

"You have to tell them you gave the cigarette to me," pleaded Felipe.

"No way! No way would I do that! Just tell them the

truth," Thomas said and stormed back out of the closet.

Before Felipe could call after him or stop him, he heard the skeleton say, "I'll keep your se'cret for 'a s'in."

"All right!" Felipe said, desperately. "What would you have me do?"

"Push him."

Thomas was making his way across the bedroom towards the door to the hall when Felipe caught him. Felipe shoved him and Thomas stumbled forward. After hitting his head against the door, Thomas fell to the floor. There, he didn't move. He didn't even seem to be breathing.

"Goodness! What happened?" Felipe's mother demanded when she opened the door to see Thomas on the floor.

"H-h-he tripped," Felipe lied.

"We have to call the police," his mother said to his father. "And an ambulance!"

After Thomas was carried away on a stretcher, a police officer came in and asked Felipe's parents some questions. Felipe would be the next one to be questioned, he knew. The cop would know he was a liar. He wanted to run—to hide! Sneaking back into the closet, he closed the door behind him to find the skeleton waiting for him.

Felipe was panicking now. He was going to go to jail!

"I'll keep your se'cret for your skin," the skeleton said.

"All right—" Felipe said before he realized the skeleton had said something different this time. It was too late. He had already agreed. He went to the closet door to escape, but it wouldn't open. The skeleton was on him before he could scream. Even without muscles the skeleton was strong... Only the skeleton did have

5

muscles now. It was Felipe who did not. The skeleton had eyes and hair and skin now, too! Felipe's eyes and hair and skin. It was Felipe who was now the skeleton. The former skeleton finished pulling up the skin of Felipe's legs as if it was a pair of jeans. Felipe watched with hollow eye sockets as the thief stuffed the last of his guts into a flap of belly it then sealed shut. Then his world went dark as a coat was tossed over his skull. A few more coats were tossed on him until he was buried under a pile of coats.

Felipe then realized that he'd likely never see the sun again. He'd cry, but the skeleton from the closet had stolen his tear ducts. He knew that the freshly skinned skeleton would do anything to keep Felipe a secret. He'd probably even skin his parents, if they figured out that it wasn't the real Felipe beneath their son's skin. He might enjoy a different skin for each day of the week.

Suddenly, that F in math didn't seem so terrible.

BENEATH THE BATHTUB

Thomas enjoyed baths—the water, the bubbles, the toys! With his duck float around his waist there was nothing scary that could grab him, unlike in the deep water of an ocean, lake, or even the deep pool at school, which was said to be home to a great white shark. Thomas was safe. He thought that, at least... until *it* happened.

It was a school night and Thomas was taking a bath after finishing all of his homework. He was playing with his favorite toy pirate ship and a new rubber duck. In his imagination, Captain Bluebeard was exploring the bubble islands with his first mate, a rubber duck.

Thomas's mother and father had gone out to do some grocery shopping, so he was all alone. He likely wouldn't have been as frightened as he was if his parents had been home. He'd have probably thought it was his parents calling him from downstairs when he heard the muffled voice. But it wasn't from downstairs. The voice that said, "I want to play," came from the bathtub drain! A wet and longing voice—it was muffled by the plug and the water, but Thomas heard it again.

It said, "Please let me play."

Thomas scooted to the far side of the tub, furthest

from the drain plug and the voice. He was too scared to do anything. The smart thing to do would have been to get out of the tub and hide under his bed covers, he thought, but he stayed in the fast cooling water, paralyzed with fear.

"I know you can hear me," the voice said. "I want to play, too."

Finally, Thomas worked up the courage to speak. He said, "Where are you?" It was the more important question at the moment; more important than asking who it was beneath the bathtub.

"Down here, silly," said the muffled voice. "Shh! Don't tell mommy."

"Down where?" Thomas looked, searching madly for a speaker or some other explanation for the voice. Surely this voice was not in the drain. It was then that he heard scratching along the bottom of the tub.

"Come play," said the voice and it sounded scary now, like a fountain of water came out of its mouth when it spoke instead of air.

"I'm done playing!" Thomas cried. "Who are you?"

"Why, I'm Tommy," said the voice, thick with water. "Mommy didn't like me playing in the tub."

"But my name is Tom. Thomas. My mom calls me Tommy."

"We're both Tommy, silly," the voice said and laughed.

The scratching at the bottom of the tub moved towards the drain plug. After a moment of quiet, the drain plug moved up. The thing under the tub was poking it! Poke. Poke. Poke. Thomas wanted to rush over and push it back down, but he was still frozen in terror. Water suddenly started rushing down the drain. Captain

Bluebeard steered his ship into the whirlpool and disappeared down the drain, and the new rubber duck followed. After the water had drained completely, Thomas stood up. It appeared the owner of the voice, Tommy, had disappeared just as quickly as he came. Thomas grabbed his towel to dry off.

Then he heard the squeak from the new rubber duck.

Squeak, squeak, squeak.

His heart dropped into the pit of his stomach.

"We haven't finished playing yet," said the voice and it was clearer now that the water was gone. "Mommy didn't like me playing."

"Maybe we shouldn't play then," Thomas said and since the voice cared very much what its mother thought, he added, "Mommy wouldn't like it if we did."

"No. Mommy doesn't like playing," the voice said, sadly. "Is mother there?"

"No."

"Then we can play!"

Thomas moved closer to the drain and peeked down it. He saw blackness and the faint shine of light reflecting off of water, and an eye. Yes, an eye was looking up at him!

"What if she catches us?" Thomas said, very much not wanting to play with the thing beneath the tub. He thought if he scared the owner of the voice into thinking its mother would find out, it would just leave him alone.

"There's no water left," the voice said. "She can't drown you if there's no water and she can't kill me twice. So we can play all night!"

"She drowned you?"

"She didn't like me playing in the tub," the voice

sobbed. "Wait—" The voice paused as if it heard something. Thomas too heard something. The front door. His father and mother were home. At least he hoped it was them... It could be the voice's mother.

The voice said, "Mommy says to go to bed. I'll give your toys back next time you take a bath."

A knock at the bathroom door made Thomas jump. His mother's voice called through the door, "Don't be playing around in there, Tommy."

Thomas never took a bath again despite his parents and friends pleading him to. His mother wanted him to bathe most of all.

"Better dirty than dead," he'd always say until he got an infection from the filth and died.

I NEED A VOLUNTEER

In elementary school I had the meanest of all teachers. Mrs. Poole was supposedly a magician, so everyone was excited on the first day of school; but she walked in looking mean and angry. She was as cruel as she was ugly so we knew right away what we were getting—it wasn't magical. The huge wart on her crooked nose shined with grease. The rest of her body looked boiled and nearly purple. Her fingers were knotted and her spine twisted like an old tree. Hunching over her students, she'd yell at any kid who asked to use the restroom. Those who didn't know an answer to a math problem didn't get to go to recess. When she caught one girl talking to another, she gave the whole class detention.

It was in detention after school that she first smiled her hideous smile. I swear I saw a spider run across her teeth and slip into the gap where she was missing a tooth.

When Mrs. Poole suggested we let her do a magic show, we all excitedly agreed. She started with pulling a string of handkerchiefs from her pocket. They were seemingly endless, but she stopped when they all started coming out red. Stuffing the string of cloths back into her pockets, she used the last few to wipe up some red liquid that had dripped to the floor. Then she pocketed those, too.

Next she called for a volunteer. The class bully raised his hand along with most of the class. I think he wanted to ruin her next trick, though, to make her mad. Mrs. Poole chose him and had him climb into a large trunk, which she then locked him inside.

"I'm going to make him disappear," Mrs. Poole said. She chanted some hocus pocus and tapped a wand on the top of the chest. Then to prove that he had disappeared, she took a jar of black widow spiders and tossed them into the chest. Only a few of us saw the chest jerk and fewer still heard a muffled shriek.

One of the girls who had talked earlier and got us all detention raised her hand.

"Yes, dear?" Mrs. Poole said.

"Are you going to bring him back?" the girl asked.

"He's very good at this disappearing trick. He'll return when he's ready, but he's very good at this. We might never find him," the teacher said with a smirk. "I need another volunteer."

We were all more hesitant now. Only half of us raised our hands. She chose a very shy girl. Pinching the girl's ear, Mrs. Poole said she was going to take it. And she did. She showed the whole class and we were amazed at how real the ear looked. Then blood leaked through Mrs. Poole's fingers. Looking to the shy girl, we saw her crying and holding the side of her head. She ran out of the room.

"Go see the nurse," Mrs. Poole called after her and laughed as she wheeled a long narrow box out on wheels. She said, "I need another victim—I mean— volunteer!"

This time none of us raised our hands. She called on the girl who had asked about the bully. Dragging her feet, the girl went up. Mrs. Poole had her climb into the narrow box. Only the girl's head and feet stuck out.

"I will cut this girl in two!" Mrs. Poole exclaimed. She pulled out a rusty saw and began sawing away at the box. Midway through the girl started screaming and shaking violently.

It was then that the classroom door burst open. At the door was the shy girl with one ear, the school nurse, and the principal. The principal said, "You're not Mrs. Poole!"

"No," the Mrs. Poole imposter said, faking a guilty look. She dropped the rusty saw, ran to the spider filled trunk, and climbed inside.

Everyone rushed to the chest and the principal opened it. It was empty! She had disappeared.

In the end, the shy girl lost her ear, the talkative girl got a scar on her belly, and the bully was never seen again, nor was Mrs. Poole or her imposter. Some say the imposter is out there to this day, posing as someone else, doing terrible magic tricks and making kids disappear.

—

(If you're reading this to friends, ask with a scary face): Who wants to see a magic trick? I need a volunteer.

A MIDNIGHT SNACK

When summer came along the heat came with it. Jacob would go to camp where he could swim to cool down. There, he bunked with his best friend, Chris, and a heavyset boy named Andrew, in the cabin furthest from all the others. Their cabin was nearest the local graveyard, which was actually quite pretty in the daylight with all the grass and old trees. Still, it was scary with all the rumors of ghouls making the graveyard their home. Ghouls like to eat little boys and girls, you see, so you can understand why this might scare Jacob, Chris, and Andrew. It would scare you, too, if you had to sleep there.

At night the cabin got hot with the windows closed, but the boys were too scared to keep them open. They feared a ghoul might slip inside as they slept. The heat bothered Andrew even more than it did Jacob and Chris, for his mother had only packed him sweaters to sleep in—no T-shirts, just lumpy, thick sweaters. To combat the heat, Andrew lay on the floor between the bunks. He was a nervous eater and would snack on jerky and fruit to soothe himself. Jacob didn't mind the sound of lip smacking too much. Chris would sometimes get annoyed, though. He'd often have to go for a walk to get away from the sound.

The hottest day of the year proved to be too much. The boys' discomfort beat out their fear of ghouls. They opened a window. Jacob hung up a cord strung with tin cans to serve as an alarm in case an intruder came in through the window. With the wind, though, the tins were more like wind chimes. Still, Jacob managed to fall asleep to Andrew licking his lips and eating jerky. He awoke in the middle of the night to the sound of clanging tin cans, but it seemed it was due to a gust of wind. He went back to sleep to the sound of Andrew's growling stomach.

Perhaps an hour passed before Jacob woke once more, this time to the sound of Andrew's stomach growling very loudly. Jacob thought he might tell Andrew to not eat too much, but he was too tired and quickly fell back to sleep. If Andrew got a stomach ache, it was his own fault.

It wasn't long after that when Jacob was woken once more, this time to the sound of a peach being eaten. It sounded like a peach, at least. Very wet and sloppy. Jacob heard Andrew's stomach growling and knew he'd be eating for a while longer yet. Jacob stood to use the restroom. He thought he'd have to step over Andrew and felt around in the dark, but he didn't feel Andrew on the floor between the bunks. He wasn't in his bunk, either. Jacob figured he must've slipped into the space beneath the bed where it was cooler and thought nothing more of it. He felt his way to the restroom in the dark.

There was a window just above the sink. When he was washing his hands, Jacob looked outside. In the moonlight he saw a figure and he became very afraid. A ghoul! He felt like screaming, but he didn't want the monster to know he was in the cabin. It already seemed to be heading in his direction. Jacob ran to the open window and shut it. Just as he did, he heard a bang at the cabin door. The ghoul was trying to get in!

Jacob jumped into his bed and covered himself in a blanket. He felt around for Andrew as he didn't want to make a noise, yet he needed to wake him. Then he felt fingers. It was a comfort to hold Andrew's hand though he'd never normally do such a thing. Andrew was cold, though. Cold with fear no doubt. Nevertheless, Jacob wasn't alone. Andrew heard the ghoul, too. He was prepared. More prepared than he would be than while fast asleep, at least.

"Chris!" Jacob whispered to wake his other friend. It was more of a hiss than anything resembling a name. "Chrissss!"

Chris stirred in his bed. Hearing the rattle of the door, he sat up. The doorknob rattled. Then the door opened. The shadowed figure in the doorway was huge and lumpy, like the boys were always told a ghoul was. Jacob held his breath as Andrew held his hand, limply.

Then the light in the cabin suddenly turned on. After Jacob's eyes adjusted, he saw that it wasn't a ghoul at the door at all, but rather Andrew holding a bunch of food he'd just raided from the cafeteria, wearing his lumpy sweater.

Andrew's eyes went wide as he followed Jacob's arm down to the hand he was holding. If Andrew was at the door, then whose hand was he holding?

Looking down, Jacob saw why the hand he held felt so limp and cold. It wasn't attached to a body! Something huge and lumpy scrambled off Chris' bed before Jacob could get a good look at it, but he knew it wasn't his friend. It had to be a ghoul. A ghoul with a full stomach.

It left only Chris's hand and a set of bloody sheets behind.

IN A ROOM THICK WITH DARKNESS

In a room thick with darkness,
an inky, stirring starkness,
you see the form—four corners,
like a block of night, but starless.

On the far wall of the room
a window of light is burning.
It makes all the shadows dance.
The floor seems as if it's churning.

The room is thick with darkness, still,
for the window light does nothing.
Because it's not a floor beneath you,
it's a thousand spiders running!

The swarm of spiders creeps on all,
the walls are hidden from view.
The door is black as the window now,
and you're crawling with spiders, too!

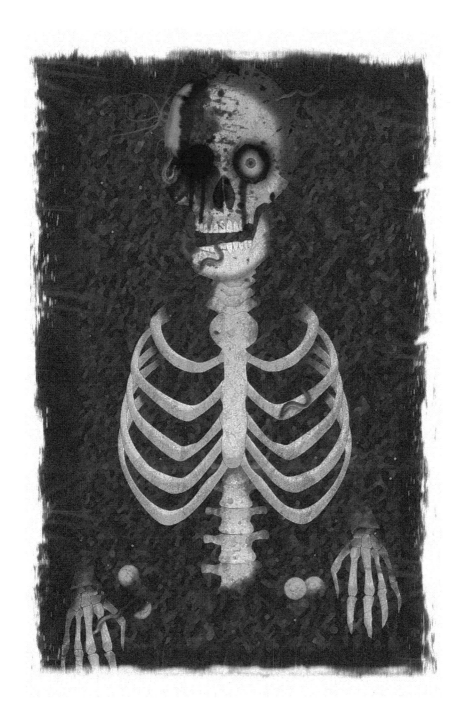

MONEY GRUBBER

This was back when live burials were common. Bells would often be placed above a grave with a string leading into the coffin so a person could ring for help should they wake up from a deep sleep, buried. Alive. Bells were made of metal, though, and not so easy to come by—and it certainly was not cheap in those days as there were wars going on and metal was needed for bullets. John, being a stingy man, refused to pay for a bell in the case of his burial.

"I'll be dead," John said gruffly to the attorney helping John write his living will. "What need would I have of making music?"

"Very good, sir," the attorney said looking oddly pleased as he jotted a note down.

With that, the two finished for the night. John's office was all but buried in paperwork because of the time he had taken off to work on that blasted last will-and-testament. By the time he finally got out of the office the sun had set. He realized he hadn't seen the sun all day, being cooped up in the office as he was, discussing the grim topic of his inevitable death.

John decided to walk home since the trains had stopped running for the night and he refused to pay for a carriage. He passed a hungry looking child and though his pockets were full of more coins than he could spend in a month, he didn't give the child any money with which to buy food to eat. John simply flicked a coin in the air and

24

caught it again. The boy's hungry eyes followed it as John placed it back in his pocket.

John laughed and said, "Get a job, boy." He passed closed businesses and dark houses until he heard a gathering just ahead. Just down at the bottom of a very large flight of stairs there was a party going on. Wasting coin on food and drink for rotten company and music— John scoffed. He'd never spend a penny on entertainment.

The city bells tolled to signal that it was midnight. The sound startled John. His loafers had little grip, so when he came upon a puddle just before a steep set of stairs, he slipped, distracted by the loud bells. He stumbled and tumbled and plummeted down those stairs. For so long he fell that he was met with the blackness before hitting the bottom. He was knocked out cold.

Those who saw and the doctor, too, must've thought John was dead, for he awoke in a small wooden box. It was too dark to see that it was wood, but he could feel it with his finger tips: the grains, the knots, the solidness of it. He'd picked the coffin out himself just the week before, so he knew it at once. It was cheap and bare. Suddenly it set in: the realization that he had been buried alive!

Hours passed, or so it seemed. It felt like so very long with so very little to do. Every now and then, John would shout for help, but thought better of it after a few tries. No one would hear through six feet of dirt and he'd just waste his air. The only sounds John could hear were his breathing and the twiddling of his thumbs. Besides this there was only silence.

He thought the silence was the worst part—worse than the cold, worse than the hard walls that hugged his shoulders too tightly—that is until he heard the slinking of wet bodies and the nibbles of toothless mouths at the coffin walls. As time wore on, he heard more of the sounds. Wet, disgusting sounds and nibbling. Every so often John heard the loud crack of splitting wood. He feared that the earth would collapse on him at any moment.

After a particularly loud crack he heard a light, soggy slap on the coffin floor. Then another, then two more, and so on. He felt small, slimy bodies climbing up his arms and onto his chest, and then, to John's great surprise, they spoke.

"We are the worms and we've come to feast on your flesh!"

"Please don't!" John said, terrified, for he could not move in so tight a space. "I'll give you money."

"Money! Money! What use have we of money?" they sang in chorus.

"I'll give you my time, then."

"Your time?" they asked, confused. John could hear one stifle a laugh.

"Yes," he said. "I'm a lawyer, an important man up there." He tried to point up, but couldn't in the tight space. "If you wish to sue someone I can lend you my ear and my advice. Time is money after all!"

"Pff!" The worms spit mouthfuls of dirt and wood on John's face. "Money! Money! We have no use of money!"

"What, then?" John asked the worms. "What do you want?"

"We want to devote our time to your soft flesh. It's the only thing of any value that you have left down here."

John had saved a lot of money—never being charitable, never paying for luxury or entertainment, or even a hot meal with friends—and now it would do him no good. He hadn't even fond memories to look back on to distract him as he was devoured. He wished he had spent the money on the coffin bell after all. At the very least.

He screamed a few times before he realized once more that no one would hear. It was then that he heard it: the bells. Tiny, muffled tings. The whole rest of the graveyard seemed to be resounding with the bells. They pealed with their calls for help. It was a lot of graves to dig up and the gravedigger wouldn't think to unbury John with so many bells all ringing out at once. Perhaps the bells wouldn't bring help at all. Perhaps the others had wasted money on them. Perhaps, John thought, not without a little cruel pleasure, the others were just making music to fall on deaf ears.

No, that wasn't quite true. The worms would have music to eat to. In any case, John thought, the bells tolled for him.

LEFTOVERS

Clyde had never been good with leftovers. He always intended to eat them and just never got around to it. They'd go bad and he'd have to throw them out. But nothing could ever be as bad as what Clyde found in the fridge he once picked up on the side of the road...

Clyde was driving, as it happened, to get a new refrigerator since his had broken. On his way to the store he saw something big and rectangular and white on the side of the road. "Too good to be true," he thought, but there it was. A refrigerator. It looked to be in good shape. Almost new. A sign was written and hung on the fridge. It read: FREE FRIDGE. NEEDS CLEANING. The doors were taped shut—Clyde figured to keep them from swinging open when the appliance was moved. He thought, "why not?" and took the refrigerator home with him to save some money.

He got the fridge into his kitchen and plugged it in. The buzz of the cooling system and ice machine kicking in resounded and he knew that the fridge was working. It took him a good while to get the tape off of the doors and bundled into a big ball. As he went to toss the tape into the trash, Clyde heard the fridge rumble. He feared that it was broken, but the rumbling stopped immediately after and the fridge still looked fine. Clyde thought that perhaps it was just the ice machine churning ice.

As the seal on the refrigerator door was broken, a stench not unlike the sewer flooded the room. Clyde nearly vomited. Inside, the fridge was fully stocked with rotting food: spoiled milk, bad eggs, and some condiments that probably would have still been good if the smell of decay hadn't gotten in. It took Clyde an hour to clean the thing out, but as he was grabbing the final bottle of mustard he felt something slimy touch his hand. Clyde dropped the mustard as he jumped back in surprise. Curious, he peeked around the mustard and saw the strangest creature he'd ever had the displeasure of seeing. The creature had the tentacles of an octopus, complete with suction cups. In the middle of a tangled ball of these tentacles was a collection of toothy mouths. The mouths had several rings of teeth, and the teeth formed a circle inside a circle inside a circle. At first Clyde thought that the creature had several eyes, but they were not eyes at all. They were a collection of more mouths, each with several rings of teeth.

As Clyde moved the mustard bottle, the thing retreated to the back corner of the fridge holding a rotten fish head and an egg behind its back. It then placed this fish head in one of its mouths and in an instant the fish head seemed alive once more; the gills flared, the eyes blinked, and the mouth puckered. The eyes looked at Clyde— directly at him! This thing could see him now.

Seeing the movement, Clyde's cat approached and hissed at the creature. The cat then tried swatting at it, but seeing the sharpness of the cat's claws, Clyde suddenly felt bad for the strange thing and shooed the cat away. The creature split open the rotten egg it had been holding behind its body, dripping the putrid juices into its mouths. Despite the smell, the thing was so hideous that it was kind of cute.

After having cleaned the dirty fridge, Clyde felt quite tired, so he closed the creature back into the fridge with a plate of rotten eggs that he had retrieved from the trash can. With the money Clyde had saved on a new fridge, he put in a delivery order for pizza. After cleaning he was in no mood for cooking, nor dealing with this strangeness. He thought he'd deal with it in the morning, but he had to deal with it much sooner than that, as it turned out.

Clyde was startled at the sound of banging. Following the noise, he found the source in the kitchen. Blood was thumping in his temples and his skin had gone cold by this point. The banging was scary and loud. He had difficulty swallowing as his mouth had gone dry. There, he saw his cat sitting in front of the fridge which was shaking violently. One moment the cat was sitting there, looking at the fridge, and the next moment the fridge door flung open and huge tentacles sprung from it and pulled the cat inside. It happened so quickly that Clyde didn't even hear a meow. He scrambled to save his pet. Opening the door, he saw that he was too late. The creature inside was much larger now and below the first head, the head of a fish, was the head of a cat. Clyde's cat!

In a panic, Clyde attempted to seal the creature back into the refrigerator. It had grown strong, though— strong enough to force the door open and dart past Clyde. Clyde heard the creature screech as it ran on its tentacles around the corner towards the bedroom. The house was dark and silent. For the longest time Clyde just stood there, terrified, expecting the creature to come back around the corner, but it didn't. Then he heard the meowing... The meowing was peculiar, as if the thing was testing its new vocal ranges. When the doorbell suddenly rang, the meowing stopped and Clyde jumped. He thought for a moment that the creature had somehow gotten behind him. But it was the pizza guy, Clyde reasoned. He ran to the door, relieved to have someone else there who might know what to do, but as Clyde opened the door the creature came running up behind him. It leapt onto the pizza delivery guy's face with a hiss. In the process, the creature knocked Clyde back and slammed the door shut. The sounds from the other side of the door were terrible: a cat's cries, hissing, a man's screams, the swish of tentacles, and the chewing of toothy mouths.

Terrified, Clyde locked the door, certain that it was too late for the delivery guy. Looking through the peephole, Clyde could make out only shadows; then he saw the freckled face of the pizza guy. The pizza guy was making faces, but appeared to have won the fight with the creature. Opening the door, however, Clyde saw that he was mistaken. The delivery guy's head simply stuck out of the opening of one of the creature's many mouths. Clyde quickly shut and locked the door again as the boy's eyes opened.

The sound of tentacles pounding on the door began, and then Clyde heard the creature attempting to speak with its new human vocal cords.

"Father," it said, cheerlessly. "Father, let me back inside. It is cold out here in the dark."

At first Clyde didn't realize that the creature thought him to be its father. Perhaps the creature did so because he was the first face it had seen.

"C-Cl-Clyde?" the creature struggled to say his name. Perhaps it had read the name on the pizza receipt. The thing said, "Father, Clyde, please let me back in. It is cold out here in the dark."

"You've eaten all of my food and my cat," Clyde said in a mix of anger and fear. "And that poor boy, too!"

"I simply let them inside. Let me in the house and I'll let you inside, too."

"Leave me alone!" Clyde shouted. He said it once more, "Leave me alone you wicked thing," before he could hear the thing weeping.

"I've let your words inside," the creature said, "and they are bitter and cold. I do not think that I'll take you inside after all. You can remain as leftovers; miserable as your words."

Clyde heard no more of it. Rushing to the peephole he was just in time to see the creature scurry over to a nearby storm drain. It crawled into the drain, and with that it was gone.

Now, sometimes Clyde hears the fridge making noises, and though it is probably the ice machine producing ice, he can't help but wonder if it's the creature trying to get back home to eat his leftovers. But Clyde eats them himself, now, long before they can go bad.

34

THE LIBRARY IS AWFULLY QUIET

The library is an awfully quiet place,
and is for an awfully good reason.
See, there is a wicked old librarian
who thinks of loud noises as treason!

She's at all libraries, and none at once,
hidden and watching from the books behind you.
If you knew how she looked—the awful sight!—
you'd be as quiet as you could be, too.

Her fingers are long and crooked things,
and her skin is pale with the color of death.
Her grey hair is pulled back to a bun, the ends
curling from the stench of her putrid breath.

Between her terribly gaunt cheeks there sits
a slender mouth that's fit solely for shushing.
A pair of bifocals rest upon her nose,
and her angry stare will leave you blushing.

Blue veins decorate her wrinkled temples,
there are blood stains on her turtleneck.
She'll sneak up on you from behind, to punish,

if manners be something you neglect.

Most patrons are silent at the library,
not just because they're trying to be polite.
Even with their hushed words, they still worry
that with one loud word they'll whet her appetite!

Every so often there's a loud child, still,
who doesn't know the library's terror:
those unaware of the creepy secret,
and the graveness of their noisy error.

If the kid were to yell, the librarian
might come to pluck out their noisy tongue.
If she found them stomping, she'd have no issue
taking the feet and the legs of the young.

So if you hear a 'Shh!' you'd better hush,
for she's close by and in need of something, too.
The librarian could use a new bookmark,
and a stomping foot or a tongue would do.

WHISPERS IN THE WALLS

Daniel awoke on one particular Saturday morning to the sound of whispers in the walls. Perhaps you've heard these whispers, too—just as you're waking up—you swear that you can hear people talking, as if your parents were in the next room chatting over breakfast. Yet, when you go to look, no one is there. The house is empty. Or is it?

The same thing happened on that Saturday morning. Daniel woke up in his computer chair, heard the voices, went to look, and found no one. This was even more strange as his parents were always home on Saturday mornings. There was no note, either.

Now usually the voices stop once you're fully awake, but this time they didn't. Daniel walked around the entire house. Cupping his ear, he'd hold it to each wall and listen. He'd hear things that sounded like words, but not in any language he knew; or perhaps they were just parts of words. The voices that Daniel heard were so quiet and muffled that it was impossible to tell. The voices wouldn't stop. At times they even seemed to sing, somberly. The voices seemed sad altogether, really.

Daniel had nearly given up trying to understand the whispers in the walls when he tried the living room once more. Listening closely to the wall he heard a voice say the word, "chair." Even being such a common word, it gave Daniel chills—but perhaps it was the fact that he'd finally understood a word the voices were saying. This proved that there really were voices in the walls!

The whispers became clearer and clearer from then on until he could make out a whole sentence. "...Found him in his chair..." said one.

"...Clot..." said another.

"...Died alone in his chair...," and this one was more of a hiss than anything.

"He was such a good boy." The other voices moaned and wept.

"A handsome boy, too. Too good to go like that. Too good to stay cooped up like that for all hours of the day. If only he'd gone outside a little more."

"Poor Dan," said a voice, and it sounded familiar. Eerily, Dan was Daniel's nickname. He pulled back from the wall, suddenly frightened that the voices might know that he was listening. After a moment, he put his ear back to the wall. The voices seemed closer, now. Right on the other side of the wall. Blood rushed to Daniel's ears; his heart raced, his brow became beaded with sweat. Daniel lay back on the couch away from the wall for a moment, but could still hear the whispers. The voices were uncomfortably close now.

"Hello?" Daniel said at the wall. Though afraid, he thought he'd try to get to the bottom of the mystery voices. The voices stopped.

"Daniel?" said a mournful voice with a quiver. So familiar, this voice. Yes, he knew that voice—it was his mother's. This only added to Daniel's confusion. Did his parents have a secret room behind the wall? Were the voices traveling through the pipes? His mother's voice said, "I heard Daniel."

"It was only the house creaking," said another voice. This voice belonged to Daniel's father. "The walls whisper sometimes. A trick of the mind."

"It was Daniel," his mother's voice insisted.

Daniel heard a creak, then. Looking up he saw that the roof of the living room was being lifted off, as if hinged at one side. Only it wasn't a roof, it was the lid of a coffin. A coffin Daniel was laying in. He couldn't explain it. He'd gone from being on his couch to being in a coffin, yet still he lay in the living room. Looking up, Daniel saw his father as he said, "But Daniel's right here."

Then Daniel saw his mother peak over the edge of the coffin, eyes red and wet. He tried to call out to her, but his lips wouldn't move. They were sewn shut. His veins felt thick with something other than blood. He felt stiff and couldn't move.

"It was only a whisper in the wall. Our son is dead."

Daniel then heard the whisper of a computer fan. He'd heard that fan all hours of his days. He'd spent so much time at the computer, playing games, reading, watching movies. He knew the sound to be from his own computer. It grew closer and closer until it was right on top of him. The fan whispered something.

A blood clot, it seemed to say.

A blood clot? Yes, Daniel remembered feeling it in his leg. He was just sitting watching a movie and he had felt it; the pain, working up his leg. Then he had woken up to the whispers the following morning. Saturday morning.

"Yes," his mother agreed with his father and wept, accepting that her son was dead. "It was only the

40

whispers in the walls."

Then Daniel's parents closed the coffin lid and returned to the wake.

Daniel never got to speak to his parents or anyone ever again, except perhaps in whispers from deep within the walls. Whispers that no one could understand. Whispers that people stopped hearing when they rubbed the sleep from their eyes or went outside.

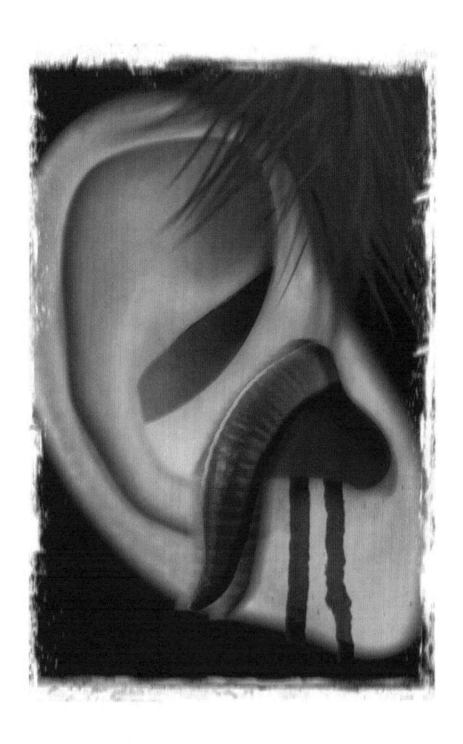

SURU SURU SCHLIP!

Young Saito listened to lots of music—
she loved the tunes, the beats, and what the lyrics said.
The music often burrowed deep to make
earworms that repeated songs deep inside her head.

She would listen to songs so many times
they would echo on and on inside her ears.
These earworms repeated the tuneful sounds
until that was all that poor Saito could hear.

'It's only music, though,' she always said,
'the noise will be gone in an hour or two.'
But not this earworm, for it stuck around;
and it scared Saito as the noise only grew.

The sickly sound sounded something like this:
Suru suru shiku! Suru suru SCHLIP!
No matter what she did, she heard the sound:
Suru suru shiku! Suru suru SCHLIP!

She spoke the sounds aloud—she sang them, too,
but they only grew louder throughout the night.
Saito heard this sound in one ear only. Yes,
she noticed, she heard it only in the right.

She couldn't get the sound out of her head!
She feared even if dead she would have heard,

Suru suru shiku! Suru Suru SCHLIP!
Only sounds and not a single real word.

The sound inched right up to Saito's eardrum:
Suru suru shiku! Suru Suru SCHLIP!
Then she felt something rip inside her ear.
Suru suru shiku! SURU SURU—RIP!

The sound finally stopped for poor Saito,
For it wasn't music stuck in her head—
it was a real worm inching itself in.
Careful now, kids, for these things tend to spread!

Suru suru shiku! Suru Suru SCHLIP!
That is the earworm working its way in.
For now you have the awful earworm, too!
And your frail eardrum is growing very thin!

It's eating your earwax as it inches in,
Suru suru shiku! SURU SURU SCHLIP!
It's right up on your eardrum, sounding like this:
SURU SURU SHIKU! SURU SURU—RIP!

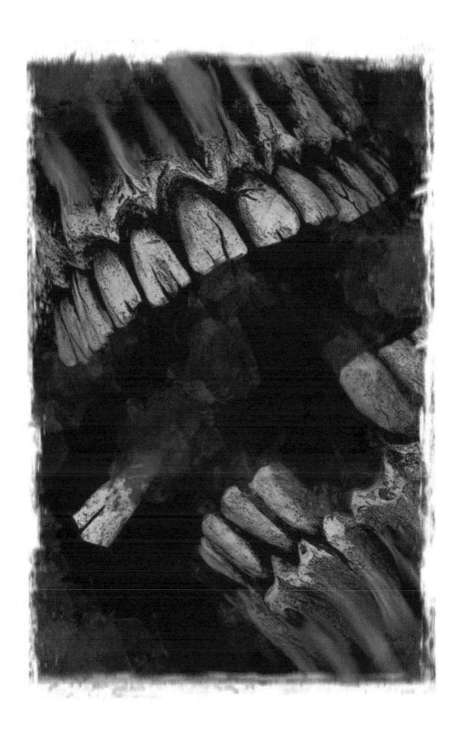

THE DENTIST

Jessica had heard tales of *The Dentist* her whole life. 'The Dentist,' two words, just like that and every kid knew who you were talking about. *The Dentist* was a real dentist, but so horrible that he'd rip out all thirty-two of a patient's teeth. Even the good ones! Just to collect more money. This would leave the patient miserable and toothless and poor. Too poor to afford a lawyer to sue the man. The depraved dentist filled his pockets with insurance money and probably tooth fairy money, too. His patients would always be angry when they awoke in his chair. They'd be ready to sink the teeth they no longer had into the dentist, but he'd move practices. *The Dentist* would never strike more than once or twice in the same town.

To believe those tall tales without proof would have been crazy, so Jessica didn't. Her teeth were sharp and important. She needed them to eat sandwiches and pizza and all sorts of things, so she took good care of them. Every year, she'd go to the dentist and every year, she'd get a polishing, an occasional cavity, and always a new toothbrush and a box of floss.

It was Jessica's annual visit to the dentist and she was looking forward to a new toothbrush. Her old one had been worn down with regular use. She checked in at front desk and was told her usual dentist was on vacation, but not to worry because a temporary, visiting dentist was in. He would take good care of her, the receptionist told her

46

with a sincere smile. So, Jessica took a seat in the waiting room and began to read an old edition of a magazine. She had just finished enjoying an article when the door opened and a patient came stumbling out. The man looked dazed, as if he were just coming out of anesthesia. There was a little blood at the edges of his swollen mouth. When he saw Jessica, he smiled like a madman. It wasn't much of a smile at all, though. The man was missing a couple of teeth. His mouth was not white, or even yellow, but red and pink with gory gums. Even his remaining teeth were pink with blood. He smiled at the receptionist, as well, who gasped. When the man staggered out of the office, still in a daze, the receptionist met eyes with Jessica and shrugged.

The receptionist said, "He must have had a lot of cavities."

"Yeah," Jessica laughed nervously and tried to read the magazine in her hands. The woman next to her said, "Glad I'm only here for a cleaning," to which Jessica agreed. This woman had her name called a short while later and she went into the back room when the door was opened. Jessica couldn't see who it was that called her, but the voice was far from pleasant. It sounded more impatient than anything.

Perhaps twenty minutes later the door opened once again and this time the woman came stumbling out, rubbing her jaw. "It's so numb," she said and laughed hysterically. Dazed. "Why do I need to be numb for a cleaning?" she said, but she apparently wasn't much interested in an actual answer. Upon seeing Jessica, she smiled. Jessica reeled back in horror. It was a terrible sight of emptiness. This woman, too, had a bloody smile.

The largest of her front teeth had been removed, leaving teeth on either side of a large gap.

As she stumbled out of the office Jessica met eyes with the receptionist who shrugged once more. The woman looked truly concerned. "Sometimes cavities sneak up on you," she said.

There were only two patients left in the waiting room, Jessica and a man who had until just then been listening to his iPod with ear buds. His name was called from the suddenly opened door and he stood. Still, Jessica couldn't see who it was calling. The man entered the back room and the door shut. Some time later the receptionist and Jessica heard a scream!

"No! Please no!" the screamer said and then there was silence. Jessica was quite worried by this point—doubly so when the door cracked open and a twisted hand stretched out and grabbed a stretcher bed that sat near the wall. The hand had specks of blood on it, Jessica noticed, as it pulled the stretcher inside. A moment later the receptionist was called back and came wheeling the patient out on the rolling stretcher. He was in a daze and, as he was wheeled by, he said to Jessica, "I just came here for an X-ray." She noticed something that turned her stomach as he spoke... Every one of his teeth had been plucked from his mouth.

Jessica ran out of there before the dentist had a chance to call her in. She never went back, convinced that it was *The Dentist* collecting teeth for money. How could she not be convinced of that after what she'd seen? She was too afraid to return to her dentist for a new appointment, or even to a new dentist, for fear they'd be on vacation, too, and have *The Dentist* fill in for them.

Over time Jessica's teeth became dirtier and dirtier. Eventually she lost all of her teeth to decay. In the end— by way of fear—*The Dentist* stole Jessica's teeth, too.

WITH THE NEW DAY

There is an old dreadful tale
of a man in need of water.
He woke up in the desert,
the day growing ever hotter.

His attempt at crossing the desert
was something he deeply regretted,
as, in the shade of his felled plane,
he lay very still and sweated.

His mouth grew parched,
his tongue grew foreign in feel.
Even in the shade of his plane
he felt as his lips began to peel.

He thought he'd make his way east,
when the sun finally sunk low.
But as one horizon dimmed,
the opposite began to glow.

With the setting of the sun,
another rose in its place!
He hadn't the fluids to cry.
He'd never leave this place.

BLIND AS A BAT

When Alex awoke on that particularly normal summer morning, he found himself changed in his bed into a monstrous beast. Lying on his back, arms crossed as was habit, he quickly noticed that they were no longer arms. His fingers stretched out with a good foot-and-a-half space where only a half inch used to be. Between his fingers now was a membrane that sloped between the points of his digits. They would certainly not be called 'hands' anymore, he realized, for 'wings' was a far more apt description. Lifting his great head would have proved to be a great effort with its new size if not for the fact that his neck was suddenly three times its normal thickness. Hairy, too. Looking down the length of his grey-brown body of freshly sprouted fur Alex saw that his torso was long and his legs pitifully short in comparison. At the end of these short legs was a pair of clawed feet—not altogether animal, nor human, but rather some grotesque cross between the two. It was also hard not to notice that his mouth felt cavernous. With his long tongue he felt several series of sharp teeth punctuated by a set of large fangs on both the top and bottom of his mouth.

Alex stumbled out of bed and scrambled to the mirror in the bathroom. It wasn't him looking back in the reflection. At least not the boy that he knew. What he saw instead was a horrifically oversized bat with the eyes of a human. His ears extended from their normal sides up nearly a foot, shrinking into a sharp point at the top. He was now some sort of bat beast.

Screaming at this realization brought a new horror. Alex found that he could not yell—he could only screech. The sound of his screech bounced around the room and returned to his new large ears and he instantly knew the layout of the room. It seemed that he could now see with sound. Echolocation, if he remembered correctly from school. If he weren't altogether terrified of his new body, this might have been exciting.

As he was examining himself more closely in the mirror, there came a knock at the door. Alex ignored it, assuming that it was a delivery or salesman, but then there came a second knock.

"I know you're home," an unfamiliar voice said. Looking out from between the window blinds Alex saw a woman in a yellow sundress. She had a gift basket of fruit in her hands. Looking up, she gave Alex a pleasant smile and a wave of her fingers when she caught him looking at her from the slit in the blinds. Recoiling, the blinds snapped shut and Alex realized that he couldn't ignore her. She seemed to be a neighbor come to welcome Alex, for he had indeed moved in just a few days earlier. She called through the door, "I'm here to welcome you. No need to be shy."

Alex quickly grabbed a towel and wrapped it around his large ears as if he had a wet head of hair from a shower. Wrapping another towel around his wings, he went to the door.

"I'm not feeling well," he said desperately through the door. "It might be best to wait for—"

"How fortunate that I brought you fruit! Vitamin C

will help you feel better," the woman said. "I just want to meet my new neighbor. It'll only take a moment."

Sighing, Alex unlocked the door and cracked it open.

"A private young boy, huh?" the woman giggled when her attempt at entering was met with the resistance of his great big body against the door. "Mysterious. I hear you're very handsome, too. You're certainly a tall one for your age," and while this was normally true as well, Alex now seemed at least a foot taller than normal.

He feigned a cough. "It's best if you stay out there with the fresh air. I would feel awful if I got you sick."

"Nonsense," she said and her eagerness must have lent her great strength for she pushed at the door and forced Alex back. Fumbling for the towel that he nearly dropped, Alex stiffened, worried she'd notice at any moment that he was a beast. He thought she'd run away and return with torches and an angry mob, but she entered, oblivious. She must have been blind as a bat to not see what Alex was. After putting the fruit basket on the counter, she immediately went about opening all of the windows. One after another she spread the curtains and raised the blinds, and light filled the once dim room.

There was a sweet scent in the air.

A great hunger suddenly consumed Alex—an animalistic hunger that took control. He felt that he needed to eat and that nothing else mattered. Despite his efforts to be civil, he found himself stalking his neighbor as she chatted about anything and everything, all of which he tuned out. Alex was right up on her when she screamed. Recoiling from the noise, Alex regained some composure. He was embarrassed and scared all at once. It seemed that she screamed in joy, not terror, though, to his great relief. She'd come across a picture of him with friends. "You were so cute back then," she said, unaware that the picture was from only a few weeks prior. "You've really grown up, huh?"

"Y-yes," Alex stammered.

After a moment of the woman observing his living room, a hoard of other neighbors came through the door. Alex pulled his towel tighter. They said in unison, "Are you alright? We heard a scream."

"Quite alright," the first visitor said.

"So you're the new neighbor?" one of the newly arrived women asked. Alex nodded and the woman remarked, "The strong silent type."

After a moment everyone ended up on Alex's set of couches. Sitting around the coffee table, they enjoyed tea and scones. There were gossip and laughs, and thankfully no screams. The sweet scent was still in the air, though, and Alex was hungry... for his guests, he thought in horror. He sniffed and it seemed the smell came from the first neighbor to have greeted him and he found himself looming over her, salivating. With a squeal she grabbed his suddenly exposed bat wing. "These nails," she said, pulling a file from her purse, "Poor state."

As she filed his nails, two of his other guests, in what he could only imagine was a bid for his attention, massaged his head and feet. It felt so nice that he hardly noticed when the towel fell off, revealing his pointy ears. The guests didn't respond in terror to his large bat ears or clawed feet. In fact, they didn't seem concerned at all with his monstrous appearance. The fourth guest retrieved the fruit tray and held a mango out for Alex to eat. Sniffing it, he realized that the sweet smell in the air was not his guests, after all, but rather the gifted fruit. He bit into the mango and ate several more on top of a pineapple before his hunger was satisfied. Alex closed his eyes and enjoyed the pampering for a moment, thinking this new body might not be all bad if he could still have friends. Maybe he could even fly.

Still, it was all so strange. Surely everyone else noticed. Confused, Alex said to his guests, "Have you not noticed anything strange?"

"No," they said in unison from the ceiling from which they now hung. Looking up Alex saw a group of owl beasts looking down at him questioningly. Their sharp beaks protruded from their large faces and they twisted their necks to impossible angles. "Like what?"

To keep himself from screaming, Alex looked away. He picked up his tea cup with a shaking bat wing and took a sip before saying, "Nothing. Never mind."

"Say," one of the owl beasts said. "I'm getting pretty hungry."

Alex felt himself sinking into his seat as they all agreed one by one, nodding their great feathered heads. Each of his guests began to lean towards him, dropping down to tower above him, licking their beaks. In their still human eyes he saw great hunger.

As they surrounded him, Alex cursed himself for not seeing this coming. He'd been as blind as a bat. It was easy enough to see, though—with the fruit gone and the scones, too—that he was the only thing left to eat.

PLUM JELLY

Once there was a boy hungry for sweets—
thought he'd get some candy and trick-or-treat.
He set off with his plastic pumpkin in hand
with a route thought out, all plotted and planned.

But it wasn't yet then Halloween night,
and there wasn't another kid in sight.
Still, he knocked on the first house's door,
dressed up with tusks to look like a boar.

'Little pig,' the bent but kind old man said,
'come, the candy is all out in the shed.'
So the boy agreed, eager for sweets;
he followed the man far from the streets.

'You'll come back later, too, for the feast?
Your folks are coming, there's room for a beast.'
The boy grunted like a boar to say 'yes'—
This man threw the best feasts for all of his
guests.

In the shed the boy saw only plums,
and suddenly he felt so very dumb.
Looking this way and that, not a treat was spied.
Plums were not candy—the man had lied.

He saw he was trapped as he tried to leave
for the man pulled a knife out of his sleeve.
The boy dropped his plastic pumpkin pail.
He opened his mouth, wanting to wail.

The knife went up, the lights went out,
the boy dropped dead before he could shout.
How'd the idea of sweets get in his head?
You can't eat candy when you are dead!

The youthful boar was stuffed with fruit.
On a platter he was served as a brute.
His parents shared a slice of belly,
slathered with a scoop of plum jelly.

'Have you seen our son this evening?'
The boy's parents asked, their lips bleeding—
with jelly. With jelly, and a bit of child.
'Probably stuffed already,' the man said and
smiled.

A STRONG BACK

Room and board were included when Riley took the job as a farmhand. He was hired right away because the farmer said that Riley had a strong back. The farmer grew corn and Riley helped harvest it. That's all they ate, too. Corn. Every meal. Riley was tired of it after the first few days, but he dared not say anything for fear of losing his job. He couldn't even remember what he was doing before this job, so he figured it wasn't really important. The farmer and his several daughters just kept saying that it would grow on Riley.

Some days were harder than others as the farmer's daughters would occasionally go missing for a few days at a time. When they did, Riley had to pick up the slack.

The crop was a good six feet tall when the real trouble began... After a hard day of work, Riley ate a corn supper with the farmer and his family of daughters. Then, worn out, he retired to the bedroom that had been made up for him. It was a second floor room. As everyone went to bed so early—early enough that the sun was still up—the farmer had covered the glass with foil. This kept the light out and the room cool, but it didn't keep the noises out. Riley could hear coyotes and crickets every night. It was another noise that disturbed him, though.

"E-I-E-I-O," the sing-song voice began. It came from outside Riley's window. Far away enough sounding that he figured it came from near the corn field. Riley's back itched something fierce, and he was more concerned with scratching it than with the voice. So he ignored the sing-song voice. Pulling the covers tight, he closed his eyes, hoping he wouldn't dream of corn again.

"E-I-E-I-O," the voice sang and it was right outside Riley's window. His heart began pounding in his chest. His eyes were open in a flash. It was talking to him! After a silent moment it said, "Eat your corn."

"Corn?" Riley said.

"Corn. More corn," the voice said. "—and on his farm he had a cow. E-I-E-I-O!" With this the voice was gone.

Riley didn't sleep well. He could not find comfort on his back as he normally could. First thing in the morning he spoke to the farmer. The farmer said he didn't have any neighbors, certainly none that would come calling in the night. He said that there wasn't any use in asking questions. The idea that it was all a dream occurred to Riley and he figured that's all it was. His new corn diet was perhaps messing with him. It had to be. The voice was right outside the window, after all, and the window was fifteen feet up from the ground.

The itching on his back was not a dream. He knew that. He scratched it all morning with no relief.

As Riley ate his breakfast of corn pancakes and cornbread, he noticed that the youngest of the farmer's daughters wasn't there. As Riley was washing his dishes, the farmer called out to him. The farmer made quite the fuss and when the rest of those on the farm came running, he simply pointed to the field and handed Riley a bag of corn seed. In the fields Riley could see that large portions of it had been churned up where good corn had been just the day before. "More corn," the farmer said. Riley thought it was too late in the season to be planting more, but he did as he was told. He wondered what had happened to the corn that was there before, but he didn't ask. It took all day to sow the new corn seed, and after dinner, Riley retired to his bedroom, exhausted. A short while later the voice from the window again called to him, "E-I-E-I-O. Come see." Riley ignored it until it repeated itself right outside his window.

"I saw it already," Riley said dismissively. Quietly, he made his way to the window, curious. As softly as he could, he unlatched the lock. Then, sliding it to the left, he cracked the window slightly. There was no one directly outside his window. Yet, he saw the farmer's missing daughter being walked back from the barn by a strange looking person. The person looked more frog than human, with a great big mouth, wet skin, and huge big eyes on the top of its head. Seeing Riley watching, the figure licked its frog lips with a long purple tongue.

Afraid for the farmer's daughter, Riley quickly dressed and ran downstairs. She wasn't in the house, or on the path to it, so he ran to the barn. There he heard the squeals of pigs and saw more frog people. Sneaking in for a better look, he nearly gasped. The farmer's other children were there, but on their backs were nearly fully grown pigs. One by one these pigs slopped off of the children's backs and landed on the barn floor where they were then ushered into crates. One of the frog creatures then sprayed something on the children's backs and another creature led the children out, towards Riley!

Riley hid in the shadows knowing that it was too late to run. The frog man stopped just beside where Riley was crouching, then looked at him with one of its eyes.

"It's been so long since we've had a cow," the alien

64

said. "We've been having only pigs. The cow is growing so quickly." Then in a sing-song voice, it continued, "And on his farm he had a cow. E-I-E-I-O."

Riley's back itched then. He scratched it and as he did he felt fur. His heart sank. A cow was growing on his back! What was going on? Who were these frog people? Riley had so many questions, but fear ran through him in a shiver. In a panic, he managed to break free. Or perhaps the frog man let him run. He didn't know. He just needed to get away. To get to a doctor. To get the cow fur removed. He ran through the corn field towards the road.

"See you at dinner, little cow," the frog man's voice called out and it sounded further and further away as Riley ran so he knew it wasn't following him. "E-I-E-I-O—" he heard and then nothing.

When Riley got to the road he collapsed on it. Not out of exhaustion, but out of despair. For when he got there, he saw that the road was the end. Nothing was beyond it but space. Light-years of stars and space. He wasn't on earth at all, he realized. He was on an alien spaceship, being used to create cows. The fact that Riley couldn't remember anything of importance before taking the farmhand job worried him much more now. He searched his memories. He strained. Then he remembered. He had been a lab assistant. His lab was trying to grow human ears on the backs of frogs. The last that he could remember was the lab filling up with bright light—and then this farm.

He didn't know how he'd escape, if he could, or how long the frogmen would keep him there. All he knew was that they'd make good use of his strong back.

IS IT ON THE MENU?

The alley appeared empty when Logan began walking through it. There was, however, a homeless man sleeping in an old washing machine box midway down. Logan had hoped to get out of the rain that came upon the city in an instant. As luck would have it, he found an awning to wait out the rain under. It looked to be the backdoor of a restaurant. The homeless man snored across the way. Just as Logan was beginning to enjoy the pitter-patter of the rain he heard a creak of a large metal door behind him. Turning around, he saw a young man in an apron at the base of the open door. A line cook, Logan thought, sitting and watching. Logan believed the line cook was watching him... Though the man's stare was so blank and lifeless he might have been looking straight through him.

There was a light coming from within the room behind the line cook and, as the door was ajar, Logan saw a small shadow move across the far wall. He couldn't see anything else.

Logan nodded at the line cook in a greeting, but got no response. After a moment of eyeing Logan, or something beyond him, quizzically, the line cook closed the door.

Logan enjoyed the rain but noticed the clouds were getting darker. The thunder and lightning, closer. He wanted to get home, but feared getting wet and worse: the threat of getting struck by lightning. Again he heard a loud creak, so he looked back towards the door which was once again ajar. The line cook sat once again at the bottom of the door, but there was another man poking his head out just above the line cook. This man—a butcher if Logan had to guess by his bloody apron and the cleaver he held in his hand—had a scar across where his left eye should have been, but which seemed to be missing.

In the light coming from within the room through the door Logan saw a large shadow move across the far wall. He couldn't see anything else.

"Is it on the menu?" the line cook asked the butcher.

"Yes, I think so. Let's wait for the chef to come," the one-eyed butcher said. "He'll know." Together the two men disappeared behind the door which closed with a thunderous crack.

Mostly alone for another moment, Logan noticed that the sky had grown very dark. The lightning struck very close and the noise of the storm muffled the loud snoring of the homeless man across the alley. Logan must have missed the sound of the metal door opening again in the applause of thunder that followed a nearby flurry of lightning strikes. The smell of cooking potatoes and carrots carried through the air, which caught his attention. If Logan hadn't smelled the food, he might not have turned around at all. The light from the door shined across the alley. Turning around, Logan saw another man, this time the sous-chef, looming a full head above the one-eyed butcher, and poking his head out above the other two. Licking his lips and looking in Logan's direction the butcher asked, "Is it on the menu?"

"I think so, yes. Let's wait for the chef to come," the sous-chef said. "He'll know. Besides, the water still needs to boil and the oven is not quite heated, yet."

Logan felt that he couldn't stay there. The rain still poured down, but he'd rather be wet in the rain than in a boiling pot of water.

Logan shouted, "It stopped being served at breakfast," and made his way down the alley. Looking back he saw the three kitchen workers and a large man, the chef most likely, approach the sleeping homeless man. Lightning struck close to Logan, startling him. He couldn't stay to watch in the rain. He ran all the way home and made a note to never eat at that restaurant.

THE HAND THAT FEEDS

Don't ever bite the hand that feeds or
it'll serve you things most foul.
Green and slimy things, and centipedes
that will make you want to howl!

H-O-o-O-o-O-o-O-W-L

Should you ever try to eat your fill
from a hand with a mind of its own,
you might get a mouthful of something
that'll make you want to groan.

G-R-O-o-O-o-O-o-O-A-N

The hand might feed you some nasty things:
like vegetables—rotten not fresh.
That's how you know it's not your muscles
writhing beneath your flesh.

N-O-o-O-o-O-o-O-o-O-o-O

If it's even food it's trying to serve—
of which, you'll have your doubts.
You'll find yourself saying, pleading,
'Please! Not the Brussels sprouts!'

S-P-R-O-o-O-o-O-o-O-o-U-T-S

Don't ever bite the hand that feeds,
for it might feed you guts or a brain.
If you need some fiber it might
force some wood down against the grain.

O-o-O-o-O-o-O-o-O-o-O-o-O

Don't ever bite the hand that feeds or
it'll serve you things you just can't stand.
Since it won't behave, you'll know you'll have to—
there's no choice—you'll have to eat the hand!

W-H-O-o-O-o-O-o-O-o-O-A

With the bones and nails, the hand
is quite the disgusting meal.
The fingers claw all the way down,
and there's all the pain you have to feel!

O-o-O-o-O-o-O-U-C-H

Don't ever eat the hand that feeds,
or you'll eat your meals off a hook.
What's that at the end of it?
It's gross! It's coming! You can't even look!

L-O-o-O-o—-

JERICHO

The crows had always been trouble for Chloe. She'd try to grow corn in her garden to eat and find only cobs, as the crows had already picked all the kernels off. She'd plant basil and parsley and sage for cooking and they'd eat the seeds and the sprouts. If Chloe planted witch hazel and nettles and hemlock, the crows would tear them up and pile them at her doorstep as if to say, "plant something we can eat!"

Chloe would eat her dinner, looking out the window to see the crows eating theirs: her crops. One late summer day Chloe had had enough! It would be autumn soon and she wanted something to harvest. She went into her closet and chose an old pair of pants and a tattered shirt that was no good for wearing. With straw, she stuffed the pants and then stuffed the shirt to make a body for her scarecrow. The face was the hardest. She took a large ripe pumpkin and a large knife and carved out two eyes, but they were triangles and slanted in a way that made the face look angry. Then she cut a nose into the middle and it looked to be snarling. Finally, she carved a mouth into the angry face. Though she'd meant to carve a smile, it came out straight. No expression, but with the angry eyes and snarling nose, the face still looked angry. She figured, *all the better to scare those pesky crows.* So she hung the scarecrow on a pole in the middle of her garden.

Chloe called the scarecrow Jericho.

Jericho worked hard. He scared the crows away. Chloe ate her dinner and saw that the crows went hungry. In fact, for the full first day she didn't see them at all. After that, they returned, but wouldn't come into her garden. She'd eat her dinner and they'd lick their beaks, but not her crops. Instead they'd line up on the fence and stare at Jericho. Chloe didn't know why; Jericho just stood there, after all, looking at her eat her dinner.

One day Chloe came home from running errands and didn't see Jericho in the middle of the garden. She thought he had fallen down, but when she went to pick him back up, she saw that he hadn't fallen. He was standing in the corner, facing the fence; just standing there with slumped straw shoulders and his tattered plaid shirt. He was standing without his pole, though. Chloe thought that surely it was just a strong wind that had blown him over there, so she put him back up on his pole.

Later, in the middle of the night, Chloe heard a thump followed by a loud clattering sound. Shaking, she got a flashlight and went to look in the kitchen since that was where the sound had come from. In the kitchen, she saw that the knife drawer had been pulled out and the utensils lay scattered on the floor. This was the thud that had woken her. A large knife was missing, she noticed. In its place was a small bundle of straw. She followed a trail of loose straw from the kitchen to the garden. There, she noticed that Jericho was off of his pole again. Chloe found him in the corner of the garden again, just standing there. This time only one of his straw shoulders was slumped. The other was raised and in the old gardening glove that was his hand was the missing kitchen knife.

Chloe thought surely this must be a joke that a friend was playing on her.

She went to Jericho and as she was putting him back up on his pole again, she wondered, "Who has been messing with you, poor Jericho?"

Chloe had not meant to get an answer, but she got one. The scarecrow said, "It is nice to hear your voice, great gardener." Chloe leapt back and saw that Jericho's straight mouth had twisted into a grin. "I cut myself some ear holes so that I can hear you calling," the voice came from Jericho's pumpkin head. "Surely you've called me to dinner and I simply haven't heard."

Chloe looked horrified, as she *was* horrified. She didn't say anything.

"Why don't you smile, great gardener? Shall I cut a smile for you?"

Chloe screamed and stumbled back as Jericho leapt off his pole and slashed at her with the knife. Scrambling, she got up and rushed inside her house and closed the door.

Jericho followed and scraped the knife against the door. "Surely you just forgot to invite me in for dinner, great gardener. Let me carve some manners into you!"

The sun was coming up and still Jericho scraped his knife at the door.

"Great gardener, I'm hungry. Surely you'll have me in for dinner."

Now the sun had risen and the crows were cawing and Chloe got an idea. She grabbed a bag of seeds and a can of corn and when Jericho said once more, "Surely you will have me for dinner!" Chloe opened the door and threw the seed and corn at Jericho, covering him from his pumpkin head to his straw feet. In an instant he was

76

covered in hungry crows that had flown to him from the fence that they were watching from.

"How about we have you for breakfast?" Chloe said and Jericho was gone, in the bellies of three-dozen crows.

She thought it was over then, but it wasn't. For in the corner Jericho kept on going to when he had left his pole, Chloe found a pumpkin. Turning it around, she saw that Jericho had been carving a face for a scarecrow friend. As she went to smash it, she heard something. A quiet whisper. The words were so quiet that they were impossible to understand. Leaning closer, the words still were not clear. Chloe had to place the pumpkin all the way on her head to hear the words over the cawing of the crows.

They said, "Hello, great gardener. How nice of you to join me."

A week passed before Chloe's friends came by looking for her. She was nowhere to be seen. There was only a pumpkin-headed scarecrow in the middle of the garden, working hard to keep the crows away.

THE DEEP

Emma couldn't remember exactly how she got to the deep water. She simply awoke surrounded by water on all sides. Above, there was only darkness: a starless night. It must have been a new moon, she thought, with little comfort. The pitch black only added to her confusion. Emma could hardly make out her own limbs. Looking down she realized that her feet had disappeared beneath her inflatable ring float. She kicked in search of something to stand on—a sand bed or boulder—but felt only cold water. Lots and lots of water.

Panicking then, Emma thrashed about. She kicked wildly, but only managed to move herself in circles. When her ring float threaten to tip over, she stopped kicking. If it flipped she would surely drown, as she wasn't a strong swimmer. Calming herself, she listened for movement but heard only the ripples she herself made with her bobbing—up and down. She twisted gently this way and that way looking for a light that might be from a lighthouse or a coast guard boat, but she saw nothing. Several minutes passed in silence until she heard ripples from further out.

Something was in the water with her!

"Hello?" Emma said, her voice quivering.

She heard bubbles and then more ripples, this time from behind her.

"Hello?" she said again. "Is anyone there?"

Something brushed against her leg. Just then whatever it was—a creature, she could only imagine—breached in front of her and even in the dimness she could see the flash of what appeared to be the white of wide eyes. It was a brief flash, but Emma was confident that the set of eyes were set in a human distance apart from one another. Someone was in the water with her.

"Who's there?" she demanded to know, though she was in no position to demand anything. She was simply compelled by fear to make herself seem up for a fight. "Who are you?"

"Me?" said a throaty voice. It surprised Emma in its nearness, as if it were just beside her. "Not me. We. We are the Deep."

"The Deep?"

Several more voices moaned from several feet away, their number seemingly enough to surround Emma, though she could not see them. Their voices, too, were throaty and deep, with some a little shrill and haunting. The closest of the voices chuckled a deep, throaty chuckle—the most solid thing around. Then all went quiet until Emma yelped. She had felt a nibble at her foot. The Deep surfaced once more and chuckled again.

"What do you want?" Emma shrieked.

"Not much." The way the voice snapped its teeth between words made it seem like it was a great white shark or a hungry alligator, but those didn't talk. This had to be human. Emma dared not allow herself to think that it could be something worse. "We want simply to have company."

The Deep yawned—a wave of yawns from a circle all around Emma.

"Company?" Emma asked, fearing clarification.

"We want your company. Down below."

"But I can't breathe underwater," Emma said in a flurry of tongue and lips.

"Then we won't expect you to speak." It said. "Just to listen."

Emma said nothing as she heard the sound of something from further out. A haunting song of loss from all the throaty mouths of The Deep.

"We're so tired," the voices of The Deep yawned in unison, then, to Emma's relief: "We'll just have to invite you down in the morning."

"Yes," Emma said. "I don't want to put you out."

"See you in the morning," the voices said and disappeared with a great many splashes of water. Alone, Emma shook with fear. She wondered how many hours she had until dawn; how many more hours she had to breathe. It seemed an hour or so passed before she heard anything besides her own heavy breathing.

"—I just love kids," a deep male voice said. It sounded like coach Wilkins talking. As the voice grew nearer, it sounded as if it was walking on solid ground, not wading through water. Beyond confused, Emma remained silent, fearful that it was the creature or madness playing a trick on her. "After you, my dear," the male voice said. "I'm just going to go get our candle lit dinner from the microwave."

The voice that answered sounded like Emma's math teacher, Miss Smalls. The voice said, "That sounds lovely. It's rather dark in here, though."

"Oh, yes. Sorry," the coach Wilkins voice said, and Emma heard him scurry off somewhere. He most certainly was running, not swimming. "I'll just turn on the lights."

Emma heard a click and the sun suddenly appeared mid-sky. Only it wasn't the sun. It was several strips of fluorescent lights. Her eyes adjusted quickly and she noticed that she wasn't in a swamp or an ocean. She wasn't even in a lake. She was in the deep end of a large, rectangular swimming pool.

"Oh jeez," Emma now heard Coach Wilkins say. In the light she could see it really was him. He leapt in the water and swam to her. As he pulled her to the edge of the pool, Emma looked into the depths. She saw no person, no creature, nothing.

"Love kids, huh?" Miss Smalls said, her arms crossed. She tapped her foot. After coach Wilkins fumbled over his words and failed to explain himself, Miss Smalls left with a huff and a puff of anger. After she had left, the coach and Emma sat at the edge of the pool, kicking their legs in the clear water.

Emma asked coach Wilkins then if he saw anyone leave, but he said no. "You're the only one here."

"You're certain?"

The coach nodded, but there was a sudden sadness in his eyes. "I'm sorry for leaving you in here. I feel terrible. You'd think I'd be more careful seeing as that team of swimmers drowned in here years ago."

"They did?"

"Oh, yes." The coach nodded, solemnly. "The lifeguard found them all floating face down the following morning. Strangest thing. They were all good swimmers, too."

Emma told him what had happen to her and by the

end of her tale they had both withdrawn their legs from the water and moved several feet back to the bleachers. Uneasy, they left. On their way out, they both heard a deep throaty chuckle from the mouth of the pool. They both walked away a little more quickly after they'd heard it.

To this day Emma refuses to return to the pool and coach Wilkins refuses to go alone. Sometimes Emma still passes the pool, though, and when she does she can hear that chorus of throaty voices from the pool. Their haunting song is always followed by the lonely moan of several voices and this brings relief, for Emma knows the deep has gone without company for another night.

THE SKELETON CREW

Carter served as a cook on a small wooden crabbing ship. He was more of a potato peeler than anything resembling a chef, as the crew had potatoes with every meal and they took the longest to prepare. He'd spend what felt like hours peeling and peeling and peeling. The captain told Carter that they had to have potatoes. Not because he enjoyed them, or because they were cheap, but because they might serve as a warning. He said that Carter's job was as important as the scout in the crow's nest on top of the mast. Apparently, if Carter were to peel a potato and it came out looking like a skull—with the brown divot eyes looking like eye sockets and a missing nose and a toothy grin—it meant that the Corpse Captain was close.

The Corpse Captain was the most feared pirate on the seas in those days, you see. The stories said he sailed the Bermuda Triangle claiming the souls of lost sailors. He'd sometimes recruit the recently dead sailors to man his ghost ship. "Dead men tell no tales, old boy," Carter's captain had said to him once, "and crew are loyal." No sailor had ever arrived to give a clear description of the Corpse Captain. Everyone figured that missing sailors were dead or part of the skeleton crew, claimed by the evil Corpse Captain. Through heavy fog, some sailors claimed to have seen the ghost ship while avoiding being spotted themselves. They claimed to have seen the Corpse Captain and his monstrous skeleton crew sail past with howls and wails and cackles.

They called them the skeleton crew not because they were so few, but because they were mostly skeletons. The newest crew members still had dead flesh that the ocean storms hadn't yet washed away. Always there would be one or two with guts spilling out of their dead bellies. These organs and chunks of flesh would slop into the ocean where sharks and seagulls ate easy meals. The ghost ship was said to always have several sharks circling it.

However, not all the crew were said to be skeletons or corpses. It was said that the Corpse Captain's first mate was a huge beast, capable of tearing a man in two with his large mouth alone. His crow's nest lookout: a witch who didn't even need eyes to see, for she saw fear as a color and this color flushed every man and woman's face who saw her or heard her evil cackle. There were others, too—crew members. Some claimed to have seen a vampire mopping the poop deck. Others say they saw a green monster with a set of teeth as wide as an anchored buoy. Still others were sure they witnessed a pair of banshees flying among the sails. These spirits were silent and could sneak up on a man before he had a chance to scream. The sailors who claimed to have seen this monstrous crew were terrified, and they always gave up sailing altogether. Thankful, they said they were, for having the fog there to conceal them and to keep the clear form of these monsters somewhat of a mystery.

It was a particularly stormy night in the Bermuda Triangle. Carter was below deck cooking. After peeling a couple dozen potatoes he carved a potato that looked very much like a skull. Two brown potato eyes sunk under a brow of yellow-white meat. A third spot was triangle in shape and looked like the nose of a skeleton, or rather the lack of a nose. An evil grin spread across the lower part of the potato and a feeling of dread spread in Carter's chest.

Carter ran, stumbling, with the skull potato to the upper deck. "Captain! Captain!" he called, but he could not find the captain nor any of the crew. The boat was eerily quiet. Carter looked around, finding no sign of anyone. Fog surrounded the ship on all sides and Carter thought that perhaps the crew had rowed ashore in a dinghy without telling him, but none of the small boats were missing. In the middle of the main deck he stood, confused and scared. He could hear only the sound of the waves crashing against the hull, the cries of seagulls, and his own heavy breathing.

Suddenly a horde of strange, monstrous creatures and a small army of skeletons charged at Carter from the fog on the starboard side of the ship and scooped him up in their many arms. They carried him off of his ship and onto theirs. There, he saw his captain and the rest of the crew. They sat at a table, looking confused. The monsters kept offering them disgusting beverages and food: a green drink with worms and eyeballs and what looked like bat wings was offered to Carter by a witch with a nose more crooked than fate's sense of humor for putting him in this situation.

"Eat," growled a great beast as he devoured some of the goop himself. The beast was so large that its massive head was obscured by a thick fog that surrounded the ghost ship. The beast's sharp teeth pierced the fog with a threatening gleam.

The first mate of Carter's crew said, "Don't eat it, boys. It'll turn you into a monster just like them." So we did not eat, because the captain agreed with a solemn nod.

Except, over the course of several hours, one man got too hungry to resist any longer... He ate what a green monster gave him, as the monsters all cheered and howled and hooted. He devoured a goblet of what appeared to be dirt and worms. The man who ate it began to change. His face grew green and he crouched over as if in pain, and a few of the other crew members cried out in terror, "He changes! He changes! He's soon to be a monster! A monster!'

"I warned him," the first mate said.

The green man doubled over, then slumped to the floor, dead.

"No good," the witch said. "No good."

The great large beast picked the dead man up in its huge mouth and spit him over the side of the ship. After a splash of the man's body, a flurry of other splashes could be heard. The sharks and seagulls were feeding.

It was about then that the Corpse Captain appeared from his quarters. His stench preceded him. With a soft patter of his bony leg, then a heavy stomp of his wooden peg leg, he stepped into the light of the full moon, an awful sight. He looked not unlike the skull-and-crossbones pirate flag that waved on the main mast, bones picked clean—probably by seagulls—and polished by a century of crashing waves. He was a skull under a pirate captain's hat, with an eye patch over one eye, for this skeleton captain still indeed had an eye. He said to Carter, in a seemingly gracious voice, "You look like a strong lad. Welcome," but they knew him to be a deceiver. He wanted them to be monsters. He wanted them to eat. A last meal. He wanted them monsters or dead like the man who ate the dirt.

"Are you going to kill us?" Carter asked, voice quivering.

"Kill you?" the Corpse Captain said. "I need to fill my ranks."

Just then the captain of Carter's crew freed himself of his ropes, grabbed a sword from a nearby skeleton, and cut that skeleton in two. The skeleton crumbled to the floor. The great beast made quick work of the captain; he ate him whole. Everyone could hear the captain being digested in the beast's great belly. The sword fell at Carter's feet. He quickly picked it up and slashed at the skeleton to his left. The skeleton crumbled.

Carter was seized in a moment, but he wasn't eaten. Perhaps the beast was too full.

"How foolish," the Corpse Captain said. "Now I'll need all of you. I was going to let you go, lad, but now you need to replace that skeleton you slayed." Turning to the rest of the crew, the Corpse Captain said, "I give you a choice: swim with the sharks or join the crew."

Carter and the other survivors knew there wasn't much of a choice. The sharks were hungry. Swimming meant certain death. At least as a member of the crew, they had some type of chance at life. They all agreed to join the crew. One by one they signed an agreement on a piece of ancient looking parchment.

"Oh," the Corpse Captain said. "I forgot to mention the one condition to join the crew."

"What is it?" Carter asked, thankful not to have to face the sharks and to be able to live to see tomorrow.

"Anything!"

It was then that the crew member thrown overboard climbed over the side of the ship, a walking corpse with shredded flesh. The great beast also vomited up the skeleton of Carter's old captain, who stood and fell in line with the other skeletons.

"Simple," the Corpse Captain said. "You have to die."

With a line of swords at their backs, the new recruits were marched to the plank. They'd be having a swim with the sharks, after all.

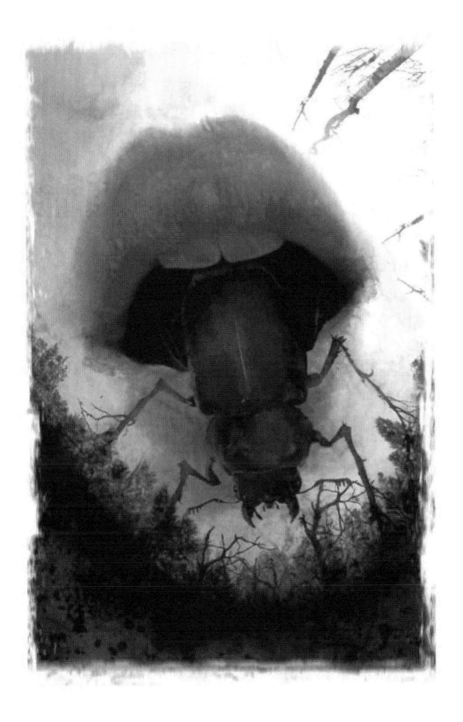

THE WOODS

"Beware! Beware! The witch's lair," the schoolyard chant went come October. "Get lost in the witch's wood and you'll be gone for good."

Ever since Charlotte was a young girl, long before her first pimple appeared, she had loved camping. She loved wandering through the woods and listening to the wind. She loved to see the wind toss the highest orange and brown leaves about, betting on which leaf would be the last on each branch. So she dismissed the childish warning about witches with a laugh each time.

"Beware! Beware!" Charlotte's friend Nicole managed before collapsing in a fit of giggles.

"Oh, stop," Charlotte sighed. "You're just going to freak yourself out."

"We've grown up in these woods," Nicole stood. "Nothing out here scares me. Bears? There are none. Wolves? None. Boars? Too small to do anything—"

"Aaaah!" Ashley, Charlotte's new friend interrupted Nicole by jumping out from behind a tree. "The witch?"

"Not you, too!" Charlotte said.

"It's just a little fun." Ashley said.

"Fun? I hear the witch is real," Nicole said. "She turns kids into toads for potions."

Charlotte disagreed. "It's rats."

Ashley watched as a tree danced in the wind. "Trees."

"Huh?" the others questioned in unison.

"She turns them into trees," Ashley explained.

92

"How awful would that be?"

"Quite," Ashley said and smiled wickedly, "Especially when the lumberjacks come and cut them down for firewood. The lumberjacks sometimes do it to help the distraught families who have missing kids. Little do they know, they are burning their own children in the fireplace."

"You're a wicked one to think that up," Charlotte laughed.

All three of the girls laughed a good while until they came upon a clearing and decided to make camp for the night. When it got dark, though, they wished they hadn't joked so much about the witch, for they couldn't stop thinking about her. Every branch cracking might have been the witch, they feared— every gust of wind, her breath. Branches clawed at the tent. It almost seemed as if the trees wanted the girls' attention. Annoyed, Charlotte went outside and snapped the branches that had been scraping the tent and threw them into the campfire. The wind howled through the trees and it seemed almost like pained cries.

Charlotte hurried back inside the tent and the girls huddled together, scared, until the howling of the wind through the treetops let up.

After working up the courage, Nicole left the tent to fetch her toothbrush, but came back a moment later with a scowl and crossed arms, "Very funny..."

"What is it?" Charlotte asked.

"The trees."

"What trees?" Charlotte asked. "What are you talking about?"

"One of you bent them over the tent to try and scare

me. Just admit it."

"Honest," Charlotte held up her arms. "We didn't do anything."

Ashley added, "We've been in here the whole time."

Together the three girls went to look at what Nicole was talking about. Surrounding the tent were a half dozen trees bending over the tent as if bowing or stooping to listen in. They would have taken some time to tie down like that. Yet, there were no ropes. Someone would have had to hang on them to twist them as they were now twisted and bent. The girls realized that they were not alone in the woods. Grabbing their flashlights, they set off in search of whoever had done it. They figured that it was some of the boys at school who did it to try and scare them, but no one was to be found. Surely if the school boys had done it they'd have stuck around to have a laugh.

The girls had gotten separated in their desperate search and now Charlotte found herself alone. In the dark it was hard to get her bearings. She had always been good at figuring out where she was, but that night she simply couldn't. The old trees all looked strange; the rock formations unfamiliar. She was lost.

"Nicole?" she called. She got no answer. "Ashley?"

Alone, the fear began to really creep in. The tree and shrub branches suddenly seemed to be reaching for her. Shadows looked threatening. Then she heard the cackle: a long and wicked laugh. It was so wicked she didn't even think to associate it with her friends, or any person for that matter. In the dark, alone, she became convinced that it was the witch. So quickly her sense of doubt left her, she realized, that she might never have had any doubt that the witch was real at all.

She felt the branches again at her arm. They seemed to be clawing at her. No. They *were* clawing at her! The trees were trying to grab her! She broke free and began to run. The branches clawed at her with wooden fingers. Once she found a clearing, Charlotte found the north star. Using the north star for direction, she made her way toward camp. She didn't make it to camp before running into Nicole, however. It was a horrific sight. Charlotte screamed upon seeing it.

"Help me!" Nicole said. As she spoke insects came out of her mouth and stole half of her words. Charlotte could make out "—the witch! — help!"

"I'll find Ashley."

"No—," insects came out of Nicole's mouth again, "—the witch!"

Nicole wasn't going anywhere. She no longer had legs; instead she had a tree trunk. She no longer had hands, then, either. From her elbows to her fingertips large branches had sprouted. Quickly, Charlotte took a mental picture of the area and then set off to find Ashley. Perhaps she'd know how to help Nicole. She had mentioned that the witch turned people into trees earlier. Maybe she'd know a way to break the spell, Charlotte thought.

"Ashley!" she called. "Ashley!"

"Right behind you."

Startled, Charlotte turned around to see not the Ashley she knew, but a hobbled old woman in a shawl. The witch! Held to the witch's face was a mask that looked like Ashley.

"Where is Ashley?" Charlotte demanded.

"I am Ashley," the witch cackled.

"You're—" Charlotte began to say, but then something stopped her. Her throat was clogged. A beetle came crawling out of it, and though Charlotte could speak again, she found that she was at a loss for words. She tried to run, but she no longer had legs, only a tree trunk. When she tried to pull at her trunk, she found that she had wooden fingers, then wooden hands, then arms. Quickly she changed from flesh to bark. Suddenly Charlotte heard the howling of wind through trees, only it wasn't just wind. It was voices saying something. "Ruuuuuun!" they said, "Ruuuuuuuuuuuuuuuun, deeeeeaar Charlooooootte." It was the other trees trying to warn her, but it was too late to run. After another moment, Charlotte could no longer move at all. Only her top most branches swayed in the wind. Though she couldn't move, she felt everything. She felt the insects crawling under her bark, the squirrel's sharp claws as it climbed her, and worst of all, the ax of the witch as she chop-chop-chopped at the place Charlotte's knees once were.

"You'll warm my grotto tonight," the witch said and cackled. If Charlotte could cry, she would.

Perhaps Nicole would be lucky enough to wait for the lumberjacks to cut her down, she thought. Maybe she'd live a long life as a tree, as if that were any better of a fate. It would be horrible with the animals and insects burrowing into her. In any case, Charlotte would only have one more night before she became smoke in a witch's chimney, then a campfire horror story, then nothing at all.

"Get lost in the witch's wood," she thought to herself, "and you'll be gone for good."

96

EAT LIKE A PIG

Years ago, Tyler was supposed to spend time at a summer camp in the woods, but he missed the bus. It was a long walk to camp, but he didn't mind it too much, for he enjoyed walking. The tales of a horrible pig monster in the area didn't scare him either, for he knew they were just stories. Still, it was a long walk. He got hungry along the way. He had brought nothing to eat, expecting a short bus ride, but as luck would have it he stumbled upon a delicious looking rack of ribs. He ate the ribs quickly, scarfing them down like a pig, before whoever had cooked them could spot him stealing. He licked his fingers as he continued walking until they were clean of the deliciously salty-sweet red sauce.

The breeze felt nice blowing through his hair and the sounds of nature were nice, too. That is until it grew dark. Suddenly, the owls hooted and the trees rattled their leaves, but the scariest of all was the whisper. Yes, the eerie, hungry whisper. No louder than the wind, it said—though Tyler couldn't then be sure—"Hungry, hungry! I want my ribs!"

Full of terror of getting in trouble, Tyler ran through the forest. In the distance he heard a pig squeal. He ran until he found his camp. Everyone else had gathered around the fire, roasting marshmallows. The lead counselor looked as Tyler approached, but with the way that the fire lit everyone up, he could not see how white with fear the young boy was and, with his teeth chattering, Tyler couldn't tell him. Plus, he'd have to admit what he had done if he explained his fears anyway, so he kept quiet.

"The regular beds are all full, I'm afraid." The lead counselor pointed to a far cabin, the one nearest the tree line. "You'll have to stay there."

"Alone?" Tyler asked.

"Alone." The counselor nodded.

So alone Tyler went and found his bed. It felt warm and comforting, though he still wished he were home in his own room or at least had some company. Sometime after lights-out, he heard a scratching. He figured that it was tree branches rubbing the side of the cabin... That is until he heard the whisper once more.

"Hungry, hungry!" it said. "I want my ribs!"

Tyler shook from his head to his toes, which he pulled under his covers. In the distance he heard a pig squeal once more. Then the whisper disappeared for the moment, and Tyler fell asleep. The next time he woke he thought he'd dreamt the whisper. It was crazy to think that it was real. That is until he heard the whisper once more. This time it seemed to come from the closet in the lonesome cabin and a grunt accompanied it.

"Hungry! Hungry! I want my ribs!" The voice said, for it was now indeed more than a whisper.

With a snorting sound it faded and being too afraid to rise, Tyler hid under his blankets. The third time the voice called it sounded more angry, "Hungry! Hungry! I want my ribs!" This time it came from under Tyler's bed.

Tyler grabbed his flashlight, suddenly convinced that it must be the counselors messing with him. He worked up the courage to look. His hands trembling, he came to the edge of the bed.

"Hungry! Hungry!" the voice said, and then there came wet growl and a snort.

Tyler swallowed and held his breath as he peeked over the side of his bed, but he lost his balance and tumbled off.

"Hungry! Hungry!" he heard the voice say loudly just in front of him. "I want my ribs!"

"I ate them," Tyler confessed. "It was only half a rack."

"Only half a rack?"

"Yeah, only a half rack. Not a big deal."

"Then I suppose—" the voice squealed, startling Tyler.

Tyler scrambled for his flashlight and pointed it under the bed. And do you know what he saw? He saw sharp teeth. He saw hungry eyes. He saw a wet pig snout just as the giant pig monster leapt at him and grabbed his arms with large hoofs.

"—that I'll just have to get some more ribs!"

"More ribs?" Tyler screamed.

"Your ribs!"

"No, please, no! It was only half a rack."

"Don't worry," the pig monster said as it stood and towered several feet above Tyler. It raised a butcher knife. "I'll only take a half rack. You can keep the rest."

CLOWNING AROUND

Joseph's friends probably regretted telling him at the annual carnival that they were afraid of clowns. Being the jokester that he was, Joseph used that knowledge to scare them. First he tricked them into going into the circus tent where clowns were performing by telling them that it was the food court. His friends lost their appetite after that. Still, Joseph didn't let up. He hit them with a second serving of his cruel pranks. As his friends used the restroom, he ran to a stand and bought a red clown nose and a can of spring-snakes that looked like a cola. It was a clown who sold it to him. When his friends came out of the restroom Joseph jumped out at them with the clown nose on. Dean and Patrick jumped and Dean fell down he was so scared.

Joseph laughed like a goofy clown. Pinching his clown nose, he danced.

"You ought to be a clown yourself," Dean said to Joseph. "With all your dumb pranks. Quit clowning around!"

"Gosh, I'm sorry," Joseph helped Dean up. It should have been obvious by his tone that Joseph wasn't really sorry, but Dean was a trusting person. Joseph said, "I didn't know it annoyed you. Here, have this soda. Think of it as an apology."

"Thanks," Dean said. "I'm not thirsty, though. Here, Patrick, you have it."

Patrick took the can.

"That's awfully nice—" The fake spring-snakes flew out of the can as Patrick pulled the tab. His face was red in an instant. His eyes were wet and he looked to be almost in tears. "You're just awful," he said to Joseph and stormed off towards his home without another word.

"It was only a joke!" Joseph called after him, but Patrick didn't stop walking or respond. He was really angry and Dean told Joseph as much. Dean was angry himself.

"Duh," Joseph stooped to pick up the snakes. He stuffed them back into the fake soda can.

Dean sighed. "I'm going home, too."

"Fine! Go home then, you wuss."

Dean walked away, leaving Joseph at the carnival alone. *That's all right*, Joseph said to himself, There was lots to do. It was about then that he noticed the figure watching him from the shadows. Turning towards it, Joseph squinted in hopes of seeing more clearly. It was the nose he noticed first. Round and red. The shoes were also red, and huge! There were ruffles around the figure's neck and his face was painted white with sharp blue triangles around his eyes and a red mouth painted on, too. A clown. The clown who had sold him the nose and can of snakes. This clown's face was not painted to be happy, or even sad, but angry. Joseph didn't like the way the clown was looking at him.

"What're you looking at?" Joseph said with a tone of annoyance.

"A fellow clown," the clown said.

Joseph realized that he was still wearing the clown nose and quickly took it off.

"I'm not a clown," he said.

The clown smiled his sharp and angry smile. He came out of the shadows and Joseph could see his outfit was grey and dirty as though he'd been playing in dirt or digging.

"I have a joke for you," the clown said.

"No thanks," Joseph said. He walked away from the clown and went in search of something to eat. He found a snack stand and ordered a corndog. When he had handed over his money the cook left to get his food. Alone, Joseph thought he'd have some fun. He tossed some ketchup packs to the floor where the employee was sure to step on them and make a mess. It wasn't the employee who stepped on the ketchup packets, though. It was a pair of large red shoes. Looking up, Joseph saw the angry looking clown rise from behind the counter. In the clown's hand was a cream pie. Joseph got a good look at the pie as the clown threw it in his face.

"Why would you do that?" growled Joseph. He wiped the pie from his eyes, but the clown had left. When the snack stand employee came back with the corndog, he charged Joseph for the pie that he had all over him.

With no more money for food or rides, Joseph decided to head home. The further he got away from the rides and game booths, the quieter it got. A sound followed him as he exited the carnival grounds, though. A squeak, squeak, squeak. Looking back, Joseph didn't see anything, but the sound continued: squeak, squeak, squeak. He walked a little faster and the squeaks came faster. He slowed and the squeaks slowed. He stopped and the squeaks stopped. He began to run and the rapid sound of squeak, squeak, squeak followed.

The squeaks were footsteps, Joseph realized. Clown

104

footsteps!

He ran and the squeaks followed. When he saw a police officer he ran to him and told the officer he was being followed. However, the cop knew Joseph to be a troublemaker and a jokester.

"Wasting police time is a bad thing to do."

"I'm not joking! I'm being followed!"

"By who?" the officer asked.

"By a clown."

"A clown," the police officer laughed. "Get out of here, kid. The clowns are all down at the carnival."

With this the police officer would hear no more. He got in his patrol car and drove off with sirens blaring to answer another call for help. When the sound of the police siren faded, Joseph could hear the squeaking of clown shoes once again.

Joseph ran until he came upon his friend Patrick's house. He pounded on the door until Patrick answered, looking annoyed. He only opened it a crack.

"Let me in!" Joseph said. "A clown is following me."

"I'm having dinner with my parents," Patrick said and began to shut the door. Before he shut it all the way, he added, "I don't have time for your stupid jokes now."

Joseph would have knocked again, but the squeaking shoes had caught up. Looking towards the street, Joseph saw the clown watching him from the shadows behind a large tree.

"Enough kidding around," Joseph shouted. "Leave me alone!"

"I have a joke for you," the clown said and laughed a crazy laugh.

Joseph ran again until he came across his friend Dean's

house. When Dean answered the door he looked more than annoyed. He looked angry.

"Go away," he said. "I don't want to be your friend anymore."

"Please," Joseph said. "I need your help!"

"My help? Like you need my help with all your stupid pranks? I don't feel like helping you anymore."

"A clown is chasing me."

"A clown? Good one. Not! Grow up and stop clowning around."

With this Dean slammed the door in Joseph's face. Joseph stumbled backwards and tripped. He fell on his back. He didn't have to hear the squeaking clown shoes to know that the clown was there. The clown was towering above him.

"I have a joke for you," the clown said and grabbed Joseph by the ankles. Joseph struggled, but couldn't break free. He yelled for help, but no one listened. Those who heard probably thought he was just joking around. The clown pulled him back to the carnival.

"Where are you taking me?" Joseph yelled.

"To dinner in the clown circus tent."

"What, do you eat little boys there?" Joseph scoffed. "Very funny. Hah-hah!"

"Maybe," the clown said and giggled.

Joseph worked his clown nose out of his pocket and put it on. "You can't eat a fellow clown."

"You're right," the clown laughed. "We don't eat clowns—they taste funny."

Joseph sighed in relief.

When they got to the tent, Joseph saw a line of unhappy looking clowns. They sat around a large table.

The clown that brought him there said, "Prove that you're a clown and we'll let you go."

First Joseph told all the jokes he knew, but none of the clowns laughed. Then he gave the can of springs snakes to one of them. They exploded from the can and the clown fell backwards. Joseph laughed, but none of the clowns did.

"I have a joke for you," the clown who had brought him to the circus tent said. He handed Joseph a can and told him to open it. Expecting spring snakes, Joseph aimed it away from him, and it was a good thing he did. Three knives sprang from it, shot through the canvas of the circus tent, then landed in a triangle around Joseph.

"That's not funny!" Joseph said, but all the clowns were laughing.

"Juggle them," they demanded.

Joseph picked up the knives and began to try to juggle them. He was afraid to say no.

"How do you kill a clown?" one of the clowns asked the others. The others answered while drawing their thumbs across their throats, "Go for the juggler."

"Let's just eat him," said one of the clowns.

"You said you didn't eat fellow clowns," Joseph said. "You said they taste funny."

"I did," the clown who dragged him there said and laughed. "Too bad for you, no one finds you funny."

Joseph was never funny, he realized, just cruel like these clowns. He didn't know if the clowns were joking about eating him or not. He didn't know if as soon as he stopped juggling the knives he'd be in real danger or not. He just knew that the final joke was on him. He was done clowning around.

NOTES

Some stories in this anthology were inspired vaguely by tales of terror the author had heard over the years and have no single source; most are from his imagination and personal fears alone. A few of the stories deserve further comment. The following is a list of stories by other authors that inspired the Russell J. Dorn to write a certain handful of the preceding stories. The inspired stories in this collection are not straight retellings, but rather similar in theme and the author thought readers might be interested in reading more chilling tales that are in the same vein of horror.

A Midnight Snack—inspired by Brown, David M. "Bedtime for Sam." Fiction. Calhoun EBDB Books, (1983).

Eat Like a Pig—inspired by Gilchrist, A.G. "The Bone." Folklore 50 (1939): 378-79; and Schwartz, Alvin. "Cemetery Soup." *More Scary Stories to Tell in the Dark.* (1984): pp. 71-73. Fiction.

Blind as a Bat—inspired by Kafka, Franz. "The Metamorphosis." Fiction. 1915. Translated by Stanley Corngold. Schocken Books (1972): 3-57.

Is It on the Menu?—inspired by Schlosser, S.E. "Wait Until

Emmett Comes" a retelling. Folklore. Globe Pequot (2004): Chapter 1.

The majority of these stories are adapted from the stories in the Android story application, *Scary Stories for Kids 2* and the *Felipe Femur* website, written by Russell J. Dorn; altered to be scarier for a braver, middle grade audience. Exceptions are as follows: *Skeleton in the Closet*, *Clowning Around*, which are both original scary stories created for this collection. Others are adapted from or, in the case of the poems, taken directly from: Dorn, Russell J. "Scary Stories for Kids 2." Fiction. ZebraFox Games. Google Play (2016) and from the Felipe Femur website www.felipefemur.com (2016).

ABOUT

RUSSELL J. DORN

Writer, editor, and creator, Russell stands in the pro camp of Oxford comma usage. He is the co-creator of Felipe Femur, a free children's website about a skeleton and his monstrous friends (www.felipefemur.com). Working with his twin brother, he develops mobile apps under the ZebraFox Games name, and writes on his own in the horror, memoir, and literary fiction genres. He is a graduate of the University of Nevada, Reno. Visit his website for more information: **www.russelldorn.com**.

DAVID VINCENT DORN

David has been into art since he could smear pea soup on the canvas of his bib. He studied 3D animation while still in high school, and performed well enough in a college game design class to land himself a job at a tight-knit slot machine designing company, as a digital artist. He's explored digital painting, web design, film, and photography, but relies most heavily on his 3D modeling and Photoshop skills to create the majority of his work. Visit his website for more information: **www.daviddornart.com**.

Made in the USA
San Bernardino,
CA